TWELVE ROSES

You are known.

12 Roses. 12 Messages. ONE LIFE.

GREG SCHLUETER

TWELVE ROSES

Scripture Acknowledgment:
Scripture texts in this work are taken from the *New American Bible, Revised Edition* (NABRE), © 2010, 1991, 1986, 1970 Confraternity of Christian Doctrine, Inc., Washington, D.C. Used with permission. All rights reserved.

For information:
Email: Piglets@Squigglesprout.com
Website: www.squigglesprout.com

Bibliographic Information:
Author: Greg Schlueter (b. 1967)
Title: *Twelve Roses*
Description: First U.S. edition.
Publisher: Squigglesprout, Holland, Ohio, 2025

Identifiers:
ISBN: 979-8-9923353-0-9 (Paperback)
ISBN: 979-8-9923353-1-6 (eBook)

Cover Art and Design:
Created by Greg Schlueter

Bulk Orders:
Our books may be purchased in bulk. Please contact us at Piglets@Squigglesprout.com for more information.

Encouragement

Dear Reader,

Greg Schlueter-husband, father, and grandfather—is a man of profound faith and a gifted storyteller. In *Twelve Roses*, he crafts a poignant and transformative tale that deeply explores themes of faith, love, loss, and the boundless power of God's grace in our messy and often painful lives. The rose, a timeless symbol of love, serves as the central thread connecting past and present, offering hope to those wrestling with fear and doubt. *Twelve Roses* is a powerful reminder that even in our darkest hours, perhaps especially in those moments, grace is at work amid the suffering.

This book invites us to reflect on the unfailing love of God and how He meets us in our brokenness. It stands as a beacon of hope, reminding us that no matter the storm or trial, we are seen, we are loved, and we matter deeply to God. This is a story to read, reflect upon, and share with anyone in your life who needs to be reminded that grace is always near, even when all feels lost.

Mary Guilfoyle
Missionary with ACTS XXIX
ActsXXIX.org

Preface

In 1976, Michael and his pregnant wife, Joanne, boarded a bus to Washington, D.C., to stand for the unborn. They were parents of 12 children, their 13th stirring in Joanne's womb as they embarked on this journey of faith and conviction. Their lives were not easy. Michael worked long, grueling hours in manual labor to provide for his family, and their modest home had only one bathroom. Yet it brimmed with laughter, love, and an unshakable belief in the value of every life.

That cold January night, as their bus passed through Pittsburgh, Joanne rested her head on Michael's shoulder. And in the quiet stillness of that moment, her earthly journey ended. At just 39 years old, Joanne slipped away, leaving behind her unborn child and a family who would forever carry her memory. The passengers on the bus wept and prayed, but God called her home.

Michael returned to Erie, Pennsylvania, with a heart broken under the weight of loss. His beloved wife was gone, along with their unborn son. Now he faced the impossible task of raising 12 children alone, the oldest just 17 and the youngest only 3. For most of us, this would feel like the end of the story, a tragedy too heavy to endure, a loss too profound to overcome. And yet, it was in this impossible moment that something extraordinary began to bloom.

What carried Michael and his children through the storm was not mere human effort or determination. It was something deeper, a divine grace that pulsed through their brokenness with the heartbeat of heaven. This grace was fragile yet enduring, like a rose in full bloom, a grace that transformed their suffering into resilience, their despair into hope, and their impossibility into a victory of love. Family and friends rallied around them, but it was this grace that became their anchor, a reminder that even in the darkest hours, beauty and love endure.

For me, this story carries a personal weight. Joanne's 11th child, Stephanie, was just five years old at the time. She grew up to become my wife, and her family's story became a part of mine. When I proposed to Stephanie, I gave her 12 roses during a Mass celebrating our love, later placing some of those roses on Joanne's grave. Those roses were more than flowers, they were symbols of a love that transcended grief, a grace that carried her family through their darkest hours, and a promise of hope that endures.

This book, *Twelve Roses*, is ultimately about what my father-in-law's life continues to speak to me: *What God calls us to, He provides for.* Joanne's death was not the end of their story, nor was Michael's heartbreak. Their lives testify to a God who meets us in our deepest pain, who whispers through the impossible, "You are loved. You are seen. You matter." And as He blesses us, He calls us to become bearers of that blessing, passing along the roses of grace, love, and hope to others.

Anna's story in *Twelve Roses* is your story, too. It is the story of every heart wrestling with loss, loneliness, fear, or doubt. Each of us is navigating our own dramas, searching for meaning in moments that feel impossible. And into those moments, grace steps in. For Anna, this grace arrives in the form of a single rose each day, each bearing a message that speaks directly to her heart. These roses remind her of truths she had forgotten, heal wounds she thought would never mend, and reveal the beauty of who she truly is.

As you read Anna's journey, let her roses unfold alongside your own. These roses are not just for Anna, they are for you. They are whispers of a God who loves you, who sees you, and who invites you to step into the fullness of your worth. Receive the gift of these roses. Let them speak to your doubts, your wounds, and your fears. Let them remind you of the grace that carries you and the love that sustains you.

But do not keep these roses to yourself. As you are blessed, so too are you called to be a blessing. The world is filled with those who hunger for love, who long for hope, who yearn to be seen. Pass these roses along. Share their beauty, their truth, and their grace. For the roses are not just symbols of love, they are seeds of transformation, given to bloom in the hearts of others.

Chapter 1

December 12 | Alone

∞ ∞ ∞

"**I** feel so empty. So hollow."

The words slipped from Anna's lips before she could catch them, spoken into the stillness of her apartment. The sound felt foreign in her own ears, breaking the suffocating silence that had filled the space since she'd walked through the door. She stood just inside the threshold, staring at the bare walls and the gaping void where Tayler's belongings had been that morning. The couch where he used to drape his jacket was empty, no worn leather boots left by the door. Even the faint smell of his cologne, once woven into the air like a promise, was gone.

Her knees buckled under the enormity of it. She leaned against the counter, eyes drawn to the solitary note sitting there. The words were cruel in their simplicity.

"I'm sorry."

It was all he had left her. No explanation, no chance to argue, no hope to salvage the pieces. Just two hollow words, inked in a hand that once promised forever.

Her chest felt tight, as if the air around her had conspired to press her into nothingness. She thought she'd known the depths of abandonment before, but this was different. This was worse. She clutched the counter's edge, as though holding on to something tangible might tether her against the pull of despair.

Her stomach churned, and her hand moved reflexively to her midsection, as though to comfort the life she'd only just discovered growing within her. But the gesture brought no solace, only a fresh wave of panic. She pressed her palms harder against the cold countertop, desperate to feel something solid.

The thoughts came fast, ruthless.

What am I going to do?

I can't do this alone.

I can't do this at all.

She didn't want to cry—she had promised herself no more tears for Tayler—but they came anyway, hot and bitter. Her breath hitched, and she slid down to the floor, knees drawn to her chest, head resting against the cabinet. The cold linoleum bit into her skin through the thin fabric of her work pants. Somehow, she welcomed it. It was proof she still existed, even if only barely.

The apartment, with its secondhand furniture and faded wallpaper, had never felt like home. It was the place they'd built together—a compromise of their beginnings, a stepping stone toward the future they'd talked about late into the night. Now it was just hers, and the thought of paying the rent on her own felt impossible. She pressed her forehead to her knees. She wasn't just alone—she was unmoored, cast adrift without an anchor.

Her phone buzzed against the countertop above her. She didn't move to grab it. Likely her mother. Again. Anna could picture her now, seated at the kitchen table in her devout calm with rosary beads sliding between her fingers. Catherine would have seen this coming; she had never trusted Tayler, though she'd never said so directly. Her disappointment was always wrapped in sweet concern. Her father's disappointment, on the other hand, would be sharp and unmistakable. Michael. A man of few words, but each one wielded like a hammer.

The thought of telling them about her pregnancy felt like a sentence she couldn't bear to utter.

She pressed her palms into her eyes, trying to will away the images, the ache, the paralyzing guilt. She wanted to disappear, to melt into the cold floor and never feel anything again. Instead, she opened her eyes and stared at the door. A sudden rush of air filled her chest, the realization hitting her like a wave. She needed air. She needed something—anything—to shake this crushing, suffocating numbness.

Anna pushed herself to her feet and stumbled to the front door. The latch clicked under her trembling hand, and she pulled it open. The night hit her like an icy gust, stealing her breath for a moment. The air was sharp, bracing, and she stepped outside barefoot onto the small landing.

The world beyond was serene in its indifference. Snow fell gently, blanketing the street in quiet perfection. Christmas lights twinkled from the houses across the road, each warm glow a painful reminder of what she didn't have, what she'd lost. Her arms wrapped around herself as if to ward off the cold—or maybe the ache.

The sharp chill against her skin cut through the fog in her mind. She drew in a long breath, letting it fill her lungs until it burned, and exhaled slowly, watching it turn to mist in the air. For a fleeting moment, she felt tethered again, just barely. The edges of her thoughts sharpened, no longer a blur of panic and despair.

Before closing the door, she glanced toward the black mailbox just to her left. At first, she didn't register it fully. A single bloom stood out against the muted tones of snow and metal. A rose. Red as blood, vibrant and perfect, its stem wrapped in simple brown paper. Tied with twine was a small note.

Frowning, she stepped forward, the icy metal of the railing biting into her hand as she steadied herself. She reached out, hesitant, almost unwilling to disturb the fragile beauty of it. The paper crinkled softly as she unfolded the note, her breath catching when she read the words.

"You are not alone."

Her fingers lingered on the note as something stirred in her chest—a tiny flicker in the hollow place that had consumed her all evening. She looked around, scanning the quiet street, but no one was there. Only the snow falling softly, indifferent to her broken world.

As the world outside settled into a peaceful hush, she turned inward, her hand resting gently on her womb, she spoke the words again, her voice steadier, the truth of them edging closer. And as sleep was softly claiming her, they lingered like a tender promise, fragile yet growing, a hope she dared to believe might one day be hers.

For the first time that evening, her tears slowed. She didn't know what the rose meant, or who had left it. But its message pressed against her heart like a whisper she didn't yet dare to believe.

Chapter 2

December 13 | Known

∞∞∞

Anna woke to the sound of her phone buzzing on the nightstand. For a moment, she lay there, the weight of yesterday pressing down like the too-heavy comforter she'd pulled over herself in an attempt to block out the world. The memory of Tayler's note, her empty apartment, and the solitary rose trickled back, each one a sharp ache. She rolled onto her side, reluctantly reaching for the phone.

A text message glowed on the screen. It was her mother.

"Good morning, honey. How are you today?"

Anna let the phone drop onto the mattress, staring at the ceiling. She could picture her mother typing the message, her fingers deliberate, her concern laced with hope that Anna would respond. Catherine's texts came daily, like clockwork —unwavering, patient, always laced with affection that Anna couldn't bear to face. Especially now.

How are you today? The question felt absurd, like a cruel joke. How could she possibly explain? She thought about typing a response but couldn't decide what to say. Finally, she pressed the upside-down smiley face emoji and hit send, dropping the phone beside her like it had burned her. She closed her eyes, her fists clenching the fabric of the blanket.

The warmth of her tears came unbidden. Her grief didn't ask for permission—it simply took her, enveloping her until it was all she could feel. Minutes stretched into an hour before she forced herself out of bed.

Her reflection in the bathroom mirror startled her. Puffy eyes, pale skin, dark circles beneath eyes that looked empty. Haunted. She turned away quickly and splashed cold water on her face, as though the shock could wash away more than just the sleep from her skin.

Dressing felt pointless, but she pulled on a pair of jeans and a sweater anyway. Routine could help, she told herself. It was one of the only things holding her together now. She moved into the kitchen and flicked on the coffee maker, the mechanical whirr filling the silence. Her gaze drifted to the rose, still resting in a glass of water on the counter.

Her fingers reached out instinctively to trace the edges of its petals. The bloom was still fresh, as though it had just been picked. Vibrant, soft, and inexplicably alive in the starkness of her kitchen. The note beside it caught her eye again.

"You are not alone."

Who had left it? She'd fallen asleep clutching the thought, but morning had stripped it of its warmth, leaving only questions. It didn't make sense. No one knew what she was going through. Tayler had walked away. Her family was across town but might as well have been an ocean away. Who could have written such words?

The coffee maker beeped, pulling her from her thoughts. She poured a mug, sipping the bitter liquid as she stared at the snow outside the window. It had fallen through the night, a fresh layer sparkling in the morning light. She had no plans, no reason to leave the apartment, but the walls felt suffocating.

She opened the front door, the icy air wrapping around her

instantly. Her breath clouded in front of her, a visible reminder that she was still here, still breathing. For a fleeting moment, she let herself hope that there might be another rose. The thought startled her—when had she started wanting something so absurd?

And yet, when she glanced toward the mailbox, there it was.

Another rose.

A sharp inhale stilled in her chest, the icy air biting at her skin. This rose was just as beautiful, its petals a perfect crimson. It was tied with the same brown paper, the same twine. And there, attached, was another note.

Her hands shook as she unfolded it.

"You are known."

The words seemed to echo in the quiet morning, filling spaces in her heart that she hadn't realized were empty. Known. The thought struck something deep inside her. She pressed the note against her chest, the other hand clutching the rose. Tears stung her eyes, but these were different. They didn't burn with despair; they warmed.

She scanned the street again, but there was no sign of anyone. The houses were quiet, the snow undisturbed except for her own footprints. Who could it be? The same question as before. The same sense of mystery. But this time, the question didn't overwhelm her. It stayed with her, gentle, like the rose in her hand.

Back inside, she placed the second rose with the first. She stood there for a long time, staring at the two blooms, their message reverberating through her.

You are not alone. You are known.

She thought of Catherine's text and felt a pang of regret for her flippant response. Her mother had always seemed to know when she was struggling, offering her hand even when Anna didn't want it. Maybe Catherine wasn't the kind of person who could leave roses, but the quiet consistency of her love felt like the same thread of hope.

Could it be?

Anna dismissed the thought. It was too neat, too obvious. And besides, Catherine would have said something, wouldn't she? She wasn't the kind to hide behind gestures like these. She believed in honesty, in speaking directly—even when it hurt.

But the thought lingered, and with it, another: Maybe the person leaving the roses didn't matter as much as the message. Maybe the point wasn't to solve the mystery but to believe the words.

You are not alone. You are known.

She felt her hand drift to her womb again, resting there. Since Tayler left, she had avoided letting herself wonder—not just about her own future, but about the child she carried. Did it matter that she felt adrift? Did it matter that she wasn't ready? The life within her didn't know her fears, didn't measure her worth the way she did.

The coffee in her mug grew cold as Anna stood there, hand on her womb, staring at the roses. A flicker of warmth spread in her chest, fragile but real. It wasn't hope, not yet. But it was something.

Chapter 3

December 14 | Loved

∞∞∞

T he alarm blared, startling Anna awake. She fumbled for the snooze button, silencing it before burying her face in the pillow. Sleep had been hard to come by, her thoughts a jumble of guilt, confusion, and the strange comfort of the roses. She wanted to stay wrapped in the cocoon of her bed, away from the world and its demands, but responsibilities loomed large.

Work awaited. Bills awaited. And somewhere in her heart, a child awaited.

Dragging herself upright, Anna stared at her reflection in the mirror across the room. Her hair was a mess, her eyes puffy and rimmed with shadows. The image mirrored what she felt: exhausted and overwhelmed. Yet, in the quiet corners of her mind, two simple messages gently rose, steadying her, refusing to let her sink entirely.

You are not alone. You are known.

She wondered again about the roses. Someone knew her well enough to leave them, to choose words that pierced her soul like light cutting through thick fog. But who? She dismissed the question as she pulled herself out of bed. Thinking about it only made her feel lonelier—like walking into an empty room and expecting a warm embrace.

In the kitchen, the roses still stood side by side, vibrant and unyielding, as if untouched by the passing of time. They seemed out of place against the faded cabinets and cluttered counter, a jarring contrast to the rest of her life. She fingered the edges of one bloom absentmindedly, letting its softness ground her.

A knock at the door startled her.

She froze, her heart racing as her eyes darted toward the clock. It was early—too early for visitors. Tayler wouldn't knock. Tayler wouldn't come back. She knew that. Still, her pulse quickened as she approached the door and opened it cautiously.

No one.

The landing was empty, but the mailbox wasn't. Another rose stood waiting, its majestic petals stark against the dull black metal. The sight of it made her breath catch. For a moment, she hesitated, glancing up and down the street. No one was there. No footsteps disturbed the snow beyond her own from the day before.

She stepped outside, shivering as the icy air bit at her skin. With careful fingers, she lifted the rose from the mailbox and untied the note attached. The twine slipped free easily, and the small slip of paper unfolded in her hand.

"You are loved."

Her vision blurred as tears welled up. She turned the words over in her mind, unsure whether to believe them. Loved. It felt foreign, as though the very notion had no place in her life. Yet, here it was—delivered in three simple words on a note that seemed to beckon her, urging her to let them in.

Anna stepped back inside, closing the door softly as though afraid to disturb the moment. She carried the rose to the counter, placing it beside the others. Three now. Three roses, three messages, each one more impossible to believe than the last.

The day dragged at the office. The buzz of fluorescent lights and the clatter of keyboards seemed louder than usual, grating against her frayed nerves. Her coworkers moved about in quiet efficiency, immersed in their own routines. Anna sat at her desk, staring blankly at the spreadsheet on her screen. The numbers blurred, her mind too crowded with other thoughts.

A notification popped up on her phone. A text from her mother.

"Thinking of you today, sweetheart. Let me know if you need anything."

Anna stared at the words, her throat tightening. Catherine's texts had always felt like background noise—reliable, predictable, easy to ignore. But today, they felt heavier, like an anchor dropped into turbulent waters. She wanted to respond, but the effort felt monumental. Instead, she set the phone down and stared out the window.

The snow was falling again, soft and steady. It reminded her of the roses. She wondered if her mother's prayers felt the same—quiet, constant, gently pressing against her despair. Maybe Catherine's prayers weren't so different from the roses. Maybe they, too, carried messages she couldn't yet believe.

You are not alone. You are known. You are loved.

The thought stayed with her as she left work and walked home through the snow. The streets were quiet, the holiday lights casting soft glows on the blanketed sidewalks. She passed families carrying shopping bags, children tugging at gloved hands, couples laughing as they ducked into warm cafes. Their joy felt like a world away, unreachable.

Back at the apartment, Anna set her bag down and glanced at the roses. They seemed brighter in the dim light, their petals open and vivid. She traced the edge of the newest one, her fingers lingering as her mind wandered.

Loved.

Her thoughts drifted to the baby again. The word echoed in a way that felt heavier when she thought of the life growing inside her. She didn't feel capable of being a mother—not with everything else pressing on her. She didn't even know if she wanted to try.

The enormity of the decision loomed like a shadow over her, and she found herself sinking to the floor again, knees drawn to her chest. The fear crept in, insidious and persistent. How could she bring a child into a world where she felt so broken? How could she possibly be enough?

Tears came, slow and silent. Her heart pounding as she reached for her phone, hovering over her mother's name. She thought about calling, imagining Catherine's voice on the other end, warm and full of precient understanding. But the thought of telling her the truth—of admitting everything—froze her in place. She couldn't face it. Not yet.

Instead, she picked up the note from the third rose, holding it tightly in her hand as though it could steady her. The words pulsed in her mind like a heartbeat, steady and insistent.

You are loved.

Anna didn't believe it. Not yet. But as she sat there on the floor, clutching the note, she thought maybe—just maybe—she wanted to.

Chapter 4

December 15 | Matter

∞∞∞

Anna had begun to notice the rhythm of her days. They started with waking up alone, the silence of her apartment amplified by Tayler's absence. She avoided her reflection in the mirror as much as she could, tired of seeing the same lost woman staring back. Her routine felt like walking through quicksand—getting dressed, forcing herself out the door, trudging to work through the cold that seemed to cut straight to her bones.

But the roses had introduced something new. A thread of anticipation, fragile and quiet, tugged at her when she woke. She didn't want to acknowledge it—not fully—but it was there. A part of her wondered if today would bring another.

And when she opened the door to leave for work, there it was.

The mailbox held the fourth rose, its deep red petals almost glowing against the icy black metal. Anna stared for a long moment before stepping out to claim it. Her breath puffed out in little clouds as she lifted the flower, her fingers fumbling with restrained urgency as she worked the twine free.

The note unfolded in her hand, and the words etched into it hit her like a breath of warm air on her frozen heart:

"You matter."

Her lips parted, and for a moment, all she could do was stare. The simplicity of the words didn't diminish their heavy weight. In fact, their straightforwardness made them heavier. She hadn't thought of herself as mattering in a long time. Maybe not ever.

The tears that came this time weren't hot or bitter. They were soft, steady, as though something inside her had begun to thaw. She brought the rose inside, placing it with the others in a uniquely crafted vase—one she and Tayler had bought together, back when moments of connection felt effortless. For a fleeting moment, she considered the poetry in it all: roses meant for healing now standing in a vessel tied to a love she had lost. Memories just days ago that sweetly danced in the hallowed corridors of her soul now loomed like tormentors; they had become sharp, like glass cutting too close to her heart.

She pushed the thought away, refusing to wonder, to daydream, to reach for something she knew was gone. The vase was just practical. The four blooms stood together now, their vividness a quiet defiance against the grayness of her apartment, and perhaps, the grayness in her soul.

She sat down at the kitchen table, holding the note in her hands. The words lingered, looping through her thoughts like a quiet melody. You matter.

But to whom?

She glanced at her phone. No messages from Tayler. Of course not. She didn't even know where he was. She thought about her parents—Catherine's gentle persistence, her father's reserved distance. They mattered to each other, certainly. But to them, did she?

The thought felt like a wound, and she turned away from it, focusing instead on the roses. Whoever was leaving them didn't know her—or didn't know her well enough to see the full picture.

If they did, would they still leave them?

At work, she tried to focus on her tasks, but the note weighed on her, its message cutting through her usual haze of guilt and despair. You matter. It felt alien, like it was trying to find a home in a heart that didn't know how to accept it.

During her lunch break, she found herself scrolling through old text threads with her brothers. David's messages were sparse and curt, as if written between important meetings. He was always busy, always far away. Paul's messages were warmer, more frequent, but even those carried an undertone of distance. She had never felt fully part of their worlds—not when she was the sister who always seemed to be the family's disappointment.

A message from her mother buzzed on her screen, pulling her attention back to the present.

"Hi, honey. Just wanted to remind you we love you so much. If you need anything, I'm always here. ❤"

Anna stared at the words, her throat tightening. She could hear Catherine's voice in them, full of love that felt undeserved. A bitter part of her wanted to scoff at the message, but another part —a quieter, softer part—felt a pull toward it. Could her mother's words mean the same thing as the note? Could Catherine truly believe that Anna mattered?

She put her phone down without responding.

Walking home that evening, Anna felt the magnitude of her thoughts pressing against her chest. The sky had turned a soft lavender, the snow reflecting the last light of the day. The world felt too big and too small all at once. She passed families shopping, children bundled in scarves and mittens, their laughter piercing the crisp air. She wondered if she'd ever feel that lightness again.

The apartment felt colder than usual when she stepped inside.

She kicked off her boots and stared at the roses, their presence a strange kind of warmth in the dim kitchen. She thought about the messages.

You are not alone. You are known. You are loved. You matter.

They felt like pieces of a puzzle she didn't know how to solve, fragments of a truth she couldn't yet believe. And yet, they were here, as persistent and gentle as her mother's texts, as steady as the snow falling outside her window.

She thought about the baby again. Her hand moved to her womb, resting there as if seeking balance. The child didn't know her doubts, her failures, or her fears. It only knew her heartbeat. And for once, the thought felt less like a weight and more like a quiet possibility.

She whispered the words aloud, her voice trembling as she tested them:

"You matter."

Her hand lingered over her womb, and for a fleeting moment, she wondered if the words could be true—not just for her, but for the life she carried. Could this child matter, even with the world as it was? Could it matter despite her mistakes?

Anna didn't have the answers. But as she sat at the table, surrounded by roses, the question itself felt like a flicker of something she hadn't felt in a long time.

Hope.

Chapter 5

December 16 | Strength

∞∞∞

The snow had stopped by morning, leaving the world wrapped in a pristine silence. Anna stood by the window, her coffee untouched on the counter. The streets outside looked untouched, soft blankets of white hugging the trees and sidewalks. She pressed her forehead against the cold glass, the weight of the previous day still lingering in her chest.

You matter.

The note's message had followed her through the night. Even now, it seemed to reverberate in her thoughts, a quiet rhythm she couldn't ignore. She hadn't expected to find another rose today, and yet, when she opened the door to check, her breath faltered.

It was there.

The fifth rose rested against the black mailbox, its petals just as vibrant, the brown paper carefully wrapped, as though shielding it from the cold. She stepped into the crisp air, a tightness settling in her throat as she reached for it. Her slippers crunched softly in the snow, each step grounding her in the moment.

When she unfolded the note, the words inside nearly undid her.

"You are stronger than you think."

Her knees felt weak, and for a moment, she just stood there, the cold biting her cheeks as she stared at the message. Stronger? The word felt foreign, as though it belonged to someone else entirely. She didn't feel strong—not now, not ever. Yet the words were there, written in an elegant hand that seemed to hold more belief in her than she could muster for herself.

The thought brought an ache to her chest. Who could see her this way? And why?

At work, the day dragged like an anchor across a lake bottom, slow and heavy. The office felt quieter than usual, the pre-holiday lull settling over everything. Anna stared at her screen, her fingers hovering over the keys as she tried to focus on the spreadsheet in front of her. But her thoughts kept circling back to the note, the message reverberating through her in a way she couldn't seem to shake.

Stronger.

The word took her back to her childhood, to a version of herself that didn't yet carry the burden of guilt and failure. She remembered running through the backyard in the summer, her younger brother Paul chasing her with a garden hose. David stood at the edge of the porch, laughing as she squealed, her arms flailing as the water soaked her dress. Their father had stood nearby, his face impassive, though she swore she'd caught him smiling.

Her mother's voice echoed faintly in the memory, calling them in for dinner. Anna could still see the way Catherine's apron tied neatly at the back, the way she hummed hymns as she set the table. It had been a warm kind of chaos, one she hadn't appreciated at the time.

She hadn't felt strong then, either. She had felt ordinary—just a little girl in the shadow of her brothers, with too many mistakes and too little to show for herself.

The memory settled like a stone in her chest. She couldn't remember the last time she'd spoken to Paul or David, not really. Paul still sent texts now and then, always kind, always careful. David was different, distant. He lived in a world she couldn't understand, and he had always seemed more interested in himself than in anything to do with her.

Her phone buzzed on the desk, startling her from her thoughts. She glanced at the screen. A text from Paul.

"Hey Anna, just checking in. I've been thinking about you. Hope you're doing okay. Call me if you want to chat."

Her hand hovered over the phone, unsure how to respond. She could hear his voice in the words—steady, gentle, the way it had always been. Paul had a way of making things feel less heavy, like his presence alone could hold back the flood. But she couldn't call him. Not now. Not with everything going on.

She typed a quick reply instead: "Thanks, Paul. I'm fine."

The lie tasted bitter as she hit send.

That evening, back in her apartment, Anna's was drawn to the fifth rose in the vase with the others. The flowers filled the small space with a quiet beauty that felt at odds with the chaos inside her. She traced the edges of the newest bloom, her mind replaying the words on the note.

"You are stronger than you think."

What did it mean to be strong? Was it pretending everything was fine when it wasn't? Was it enduring the silence of her apartment, the ache of abandonment, the overwhelming uncertainty of carrying a child into a life she hadn't planned?

Her hand drifted to her womb. The life growing within didn't care about her fears or doubts; didn't ask if she was ready. The tiny heartbeat, steady and sure, was a quiet reminder of something bigger than herself.

She thought about her mother again—the way Catherine had always seemed to draw strength from her faith, no matter what life threw at her. For years, Anna had resented it—the endless flow of her mother's prayers, a comforting and steady harbor that Anna couldn't bring herself to reach for.

But now, sitting at her kitchen table, enveloped by the quiet presence of the roses, she felt something shift. Their silent messages seemed to permeate the air—a quiet embrace of love, growing, steady, undeniable. Maybe she'd been wrong. Maybe strength wasn't about pretending everything was okay. Maybe it was about holding on—just barely—when everything felt like it was falling apart.

Her phone buzzed again. Another text from her mother.

"Just wanted to say I'm praying for you today, sweet girl. I love you so much."

Anna read the message twice, her chest tightening. The words felt like an echo of the notes, as though her mother and the mysterious roses were conspiring together to tell her something she couldn't yet believe.

She didn't reply. Not yet. But this time, she didn't dismiss the message entirely.

Later that night, in the quiet darkness, Anna again lifted the words from an uncertain place, offering them to the depths within her, testing them as she had the others.

"You are stronger than you think."

The words didn't feel true. Not yet. They remained shrouded in doubt's dark cloak. But as she drifted off to sleep, they wrapped around her like a fragile thread of hope, pulling her just a little closer to believing.

Chapter 6

December 17 | Meaning

∞∞∞

Anna awoke to the cold of the apartment greeting her like an old enemy as she shuffled into the kitchen. Outside, the sky hung low, thick with gray clouds threatening more snow. She stared at the roses on the counter, their lustrous petals defiant against the drabness of her surroundings. Five now. Each bloom carried a message that felt impossible to believe, yet they lingered in her mind, reshaping the edges of her despair.

Her phone buzzed against the table, pulling her back to the present. She hesitated before picking it up. Another text from her mother.

"Good morning, sweetheart. Thinking of you as always. Hope today is kind to you. ❤"

Anna ran her thumb over the screen, the ache in her chest familiar but less sharp than before. She typed a response this time, her fingers moving slowly, deliberately.

"Thanks, Mom. I'm okay."

The words were small but honest, and when she hit send, a quiet relief followed. Catherine's reply came almost immediately.

"I love you, Anna. Let me know if you want to talk."

Anna set the phone down, her hand lingering over it as though it might tether her. She hadn't felt ready to talk before—not to her mother, not to anyone—but now the idea didn't seem as suffocating. Not entirely.

When she opened the door, her hand clutched the last of her morning coffee in her favorite mug—a well-worn Winnie the Pooh cup, given to her in high school by an older classmate from youth group. The faded image of Pooh, reaching endlessly for his honey pot, stirred something deep within her—a fragile connection to the innocence she once carried, sweet and golden, but always just out of reach. Somewhere in her depths, the same longing colored her vision—a search for meaning, for worth, for something that would fill the hollow places she couldn't quite name. It tugged at her, elusive yet persistent, like a memory of a friend who wouldn't let go.

And then, just beyond the door, the world offered its own answer: the sixth rose, resting on the mailbox, vivid and alive against the gray morning. It seemed as if the two—the mug and the rose—belonged together in this moment, fragile yet steadfast reminders of something she was only beginning to grasp. Her breath stilled as she stepped into the cold. The flower was just as perfect as the others, its stem wrapped in brown paper, the note tied neatly with twine.

She unfolded it carefully, the words unveiling like a quiet revelation.

"You mean something."

The words struck her harder than she expected, like a stone dropped into a still pond. She pressed the note to her chest, her breath catching in the cold air. It wasn't just that the words felt foreign—it was that a part of her wanted to believe them. No, so much more than that; her entire being *needed* to.

Her mind buzzed with questions as she carried the rose inside. The mysterious gestures were no longer just a curiosity; they were a lifeline. Each note pulled her a little further from the hollow place she'd been sinking into, forcing her to confront the possibility of hope.

But who could be leaving them? The question haunted her as she got ready for work, as she moved through the motions of the day. She thought of her mother, her brothers, even Beth, her closest friend since childhood and coworker. Could any of them be doing this? Each time, the answer felt both possible and impossible.

At work, the noise of the office barely registered. Anna stared at her computer screen, the numbers and charts blurring together. Her mind was somewhere else—on the roses, on the words, on the life growing inside her.

The baby. She had avoided thinking about it directly, afraid of the enormity it carried. But today, the thought refused to stay buried. Her hand moved to her womb instinctively, resting there as though to remind herself it was real.

She thought about the decision she hadn't made yet, the one she couldn't avoid much longer. The idea of bringing a child into her broken life terrified her. What could she offer? She could barely hold herself together, let alone raise a child.

But then there was the other choice—the one she hadn't allowed herself to name out loud. It hung over her like a shadow, heavy and cold. She wanted to believe it would be easier, that it would erase the fear and guilt pressing against her chest. But the thought didn't bring relief. It brought something deeper, darker.

You mean something.

The note's message echoed in her mind, and again, she wondered if it wasn't just meant for her. What if it was for the child too? The thought shook her, and she pushed it away, focusing instead on the screen in front of her.

That evening, Beth stopped by unannounced, holding a coffee in one hand and a bakery bag in the other. Anna blinked at her friend, surprised but not entirely unhappy to see her.

"I figured you could use this," Beth said, stepping inside without waiting for an invitation. She handed Anna the coffee and set the bag on the counter. "Chocolate croissant. Your favorite."

"Thanks," Anna said, her voice soft.

Beth's eyes swept across the kitchen, her gaze stopping abruptly on the roses. Her brows shot up, her expression a mix of curiosity and confusion. She knew only the barest details Anna had confided—the silence, the absence of "the one who shall not be named."

"Okay," Beth said, gesturing toward the roses with a pointed look. "What's with the flowers? Did you start seeing someone new and conveniently forget to tell me?"

"No," Anna said quickly, her cheeks flushing. "Someone's been leaving them for me."

Beth's brow furrowed. "Someone? Like who?"

"I don't know," Anna admitted. "They just... show up."

Beth moved closer to the roses, studying them. "And you have no idea who's leaving them?"

"No," Anna repeated, her voice quieter. "Each one comes with a note. They're... encouraging. I guess."

Beth picked up one of the notes, reading it aloud. "'You matter.'" She turned to Anna, her expression softening. "That's beautiful."

"It is," Anna said, her voice barely above a whisper.

"Do you think it's your mom? Or one of your brothers?" Beth asked.

Anna shook her head. "I don't think so. My mom would have said something. And my brothers... I don't know. It doesn't feel like them."

Beth placed the note back on the counter, her gaze thoughtful. "Whoever's leaving them seems to care about you."

Anna swallowed hard, the words stirring something deep inside her. "Maybe."

Beth placed a hand on her shoulder. "You're not as alone as you think, Anna. Someone sees you."

The words mirrored the notes so closely that Anna felt her chest tighten. She wanted to believe them—wanted it so badly it hurt.

Beth stayed for a while, chatting about work and her plans for Christmas. But when she left, the apartment felt quieter than ever. Anna sat at the table, staring at the roses, her thoughts a storm of questions and emotions.

She picked up the newest note, her fingers tracing the letters as if to feel their weight.
"You mean something."

Her hand drifted to her womb, resting there as she voiced the words softly into the still.
"You mean something."

The enormity of the decision before her hadn't diminished, but it no longer felt like hers to bear alone. The roses, the notes, the steady echoes of hope—they didn't erase her fear, but they anchored her, offering something she could hold on to. Something worth fighting for.

And that, she realized, was a kind of strength.

Chapter 7

December 18 | Story

∞∞∞

The sun hadn't risen yet when Anna woke, though the faintest gray light seeped through the blinds. The air was still, as if the world outside was holding its breath. She lay there for a while, staring at the ceiling, her mind turning over the thoughts that had become constant companions: Tayler's departure, the baby, the roses, the quiet ache of uncertainty that followed her everywhere.

She sat up slowly, her hand moving to her womb as it often did now. The life inside her was so small, so quiet, yet impossible to ignore. She tried to imagine what it would feel like when the child began to move, pressing against the walls of her body, a quiet reminder of the life growing within her. The thought brought a strange mixture of fear and wonder.

The roses waited in the kitchen, their radiant beauty undiminished. Each one seemed to carry its own quiet strength, defying the cold and darkness that filled her days. Anna ran her fingers over their petals as she waited for her coffee to brew, her gaze lingering on the notes arranged beside them.

You are not alone. You are known. You are loved. You matter. You are stronger than you think.

They were more than words now. They had begun to seep into

her, threading their way through her splintered heart. She didn't believe them entirely, not yet, but she couldn't ignore them either.

As she drank her coffee, she thought of the person behind the roses. Whoever it was, they knew her—or at least, they saw her. She hadn't felt seen in a long time. Not by Tayler, not by her family, not even by herself. The realization settled in her chest like a stone.

***

When she opened the door to leave for work, the seventh rose was waiting.

She picked it up with quivering hands, the cold biting her fingers as she untied the twine. The note unfolded easily, the words written in the same familiar script.

"Your story isn't over."

Her heart skipped a beat, a single tear tracing a silent path down her cheek. She stood there for a long moment, staring at the note, the words sinking deep into the part of her that had always believed otherwise.

***

The office was lively with a festive buzz when Anna arrived, the usual pre-holiday chatter filling the air. She sat at her desk, trying to focus on the tasks in front of her, but the note's message lingered in the back of her mind like a melody she couldn't shake. And didn't want it to.

Your story isn't over.

What did that even mean? Her life felt like a mess, a string of mistakes and disappointments knotted so tightly she didn't know how to untangle them. Tayler's departure was just the latest in a series of failures she carried like stones in her pockets. The idea that her story could be more than that—could be something new, something better—felt like an impossible dream.

Yet, the words were there, insistent and unyielding. And they weren't alone. They joined the other notes, each one pressing gently against her doubts, her fear, her guilt.

That evening, Anna found herself drawn to the box tucked away in her closet, the one she hadn't opened in a long time. She pulled it out and set it on the floor, her hands shaking slightly as she lifted the lid.

Inside were remnants of who she used to be. Photos from high school, ticket stubs from concerts she'd loved, a journal she hadn't written in since she was nineteen. She flipped through its pages, her younger self's handwriting spilling across in exuberant, looping script.

"I want to do something meaningful with my life."

The words stared back at her, stark against the patient paper, as if it had been waiting all these years to remind her of who she once was. She had written them during her first year of college, before she dropped out, before the crushing reality of her mistakes had begun to splinter her. The girl who had written those words felt like a stranger now—someone distant and untouchable.

Anna closed the journal, her chest tightening. She wasn't that girl anymore. She didn't even know who she was now. But as she looked at the roses on her kitchen counter, their quiet beauty defiant against the shadows, she wondered if maybe that was the point.

She sat with the note from the seventh rose, running her fingers over the words as if to feel their truth. "Your story isn't over." What if it wasn't? What if everything that had happened —every failure, every mistake, every loss—wasn't the end of her story, but the beginning of something else?

The thought was terrifying. It was also strangely comforting.

Her phone buzzed, pulling her back to the present. A text from her mother.

"Hi, sweetheart. I just wanted to remind you how much you're loved. Call me anytime, okay? ❤"

Anna stared at the message, her throat tightening. She thought of Catherine's voice, soft and warm, the way it had always been. She thought of her mother's prayers, quiet and unyielding, a steady rhythm of faith that had never faltered—even when Anna had stopped believing in herself.

Her finger hovered over the call button, hesitating. She hadn't heard her mother's voice in weeks. The idea of calling felt daunting, but the ache in her chest pushed her forward. Before she could second-guess herself, she hit the button.

Catherine answered on the second ring. "Anna? Sweetheart, is everything okay?"

Anna swallowed hard, the words catching in her throat. "Hi, Mom. I just... I wanted to say thank you. For your texts. For... not giving up on me."

"Oh, Anna," Catherine said, her voice thick with emotion. "I could never give up on you. You're my daughter. I love you more than anything."

Anna closed her eyes, the tears slipping free. "I don't feel like I deserve it."

"You don't have to deserve it," Catherine said gently. "That's not how love works. You don't have to earn it, Anna. It's yours, no matter what."

The words washed over her like a wave, gently softening the edges of her pain. She allowed herself, perhaps for the first time in ages, to believe them.

Later that night, before surrendering to the embrace of sleep, she was drawn to what now seemed like a little sanctuary, the notes arranged in a neat row beside them. She traced the edges of the newest one, her heart lighter than it had been in weeks.

Your story isn't over.

She didn't know what came next, but the thought didn't terrify her. It filled her with a quiet, fragile hope. And that, she realized, was enough.

Chapter 8

December 19 | Seen

∞∞∞

The morning light filtered through the blinds, casting soft patterns on Anna's ceiling. She lay in bed, her thoughts drifting like the snowflakes outside. The roses had become a part of her mornings now, their vibrant presence lingering in her mind as soon as she woke. They weren't just flowers anymore —they were threads of connection, a lifeline pulling her from the dark waters she had been sinking into.

As she got up, her hand instinctively rested on her womb. She hadn't told anyone about the baby yet—not her mother, not her brothers, not even Beth. The secret felt like a heavy stone she carried, a burden and a blessing she didn't know how to share. The life inside her was so small, so quiet, yet it had begun to reshape the edges of her world. She couldn't ignore it any longer, even if she didn't know what to do about it.

When she opened the front door, she wasn't surprised to see the eighth rose waiting for her. It had become a ritual now, this small moment of discovery that felt like an anchor in the chaos of her days. She picked it up, her fingers eager as she untied the note.

"You are seen."

The words stopped her in her tracks. She stood there on the

cold landing, the snow swirling gently around her. The note felt alive in her hand, as if its words carried a quiet heartbeat of their own. *Seen.* It was a word that felt both foreign and achingly familiar. She hadn't felt truly seen in so long—not by Tayler, not by her family, not even by herself. And yet, here it was, written in elegant script, a quiet declaration that cut through her doubt.

She brought the rose inside, adding it to the vase on the counter. Eight now. The notes were lined up beside them, their messages a quiet symphony of hope that had begun to soften the hardness around her heart. She sat at the table, staring at the newest note, her mind swirling with questions.

Whoever was leaving these roses saw her in a way she didn't understand. They saw past her brokenness, her failures, her doubts. They saw something she couldn't see in herself. The thought was both comforting and unsettling.

At work, Anna's thoughts kept returning to the note. "You are seen." She thought about her mother's texts, her steadfast persistence that had always been there, even when Anna had pushed it away. She thought about Beth, who had shown up unannounced with coffee and pastries, her warmth cutting through the walls Anna had built around herself.

Maybe being seen wasn't just about someone noticing you. Maybe it was about someone choosing to see you, even when you felt invisible. Maybe it was about love.

The thought lingered as she left the office and walked home through the snow. The streets were quiet, the holiday lights twinkling in windows and doorways. Anna felt the gentle tug of the baby in her thoughts again, the quiet presence that had begun to feel like a question she didn't know how to answer.

When she got home, she sat at the kitchen table, staring at the roses. Their presence was almost overwhelming now, their beauty a sharp contrast to the emptiness she had felt for so long. She picked up the note from the eighth rose, running her fingers over the words.

"You are seen."

Could it be true? Could someone see her, even with all her flaws, her failures, her doubts? Could she let herself be seen?

Her phone buzzed, pulling her from her thoughts. It was a text from Beth.

"Hey, just thinking about you. Let me know if you want to grab coffee this week."

Anna stared at the message, her heart tightening. She thought about calling her mother, about telling her the truth. But the thought felt too big, too heavy. Instead, she replied to Beth.

"Coffee sounds good. Maybe tomorrow?"

Beth's reply came quickly. "Perfect. Let's meet at 7. My treat. ❤"

Anna set the phone down, her heart lighter than it had been in weeks. She wasn't ready to share everything yet, but the idea of being seen—truly seen—didn't feel as terrifying as it had before.

As darkness enveloped her, as she lay still, Anna let the words escape her lips, delicate and unsteady, reaching into the darkness as if daring it to answer.

"You are seen."

They felt fragile, tentative, but they didn't feel impossible. And for now, that was enough.

Chapter 9

December 20 | Worthy

∞∞∞

The world outside was hushed, the fresh blanket of snow muffling the usual city noise. Anna sipped her coffee at the kitchen table, the roses a vivid splash of color against the gray light filtering through the window. Each bloom seemed to carry its own quiet strength, their presence a daily reminder of something she couldn't yet name but was starting to trust.

She traced the words on the note from the previous day: "You are seen." It lingered in her mind, not as a certainty but as a question she wasn't ready to answer. Being seen meant being vulnerable, and that was a burden she didn't know how to carry.

The morning's walk to meet Beth felt longer than usual. The cold nipped at her cheeks, and her boots crunched through the snow, but her thoughts were louder than the city around her. She hadn't told Beth about the baby yet. She hadn't told anyone. The secret sat heavy in her chest, a barrier she couldn't seem to cross.

Beth was already at the café, her warm smile cutting through Anna's hesitation as she slid into the seat across from her. Two steaming cups of coffee sat on the table, the aroma curling between them like a bridge.

"You look better," Beth said, her eyes scanning Anna's face.

"Not great, but... better."

Anna's lips curved into a faint smile, a trace of warmth softening her expression. "Thanks, I guess."

"I mean it," Beth said, leaning forward. "You seem... I don't know. Less weighed down."

Anna hesitated, her fingers tracing the rim of her coffee cup. She thought about the roses, the notes, the strange, fragile hope they had begun to awaken in her. "I guess I've been... thinking. About things. About... life."

Beth's brow furrowed slightly, concern flickering across her face. "You know you can tell me anything, right? Whatever's going on, I'm here."

Anna's throat tightened. She wanted to tell Beth, to let someone else shoulder the burden of her secret for a while. But the words felt too big, too heavy, too raw. She glanced out the window, the snow falling softly against the glass, and took a deep breath.

"Thanks, Beth," she said finally, her voice soft. "That means a lot."

Beth didn't press her, and for that, Anna was grateful. They talked about other things instead—work, Christmas plans, the strange quiet of the city this time of year. But as Anna listened, she felt the words she hadn't spoken pressing against her heart, waiting for their moment.

When she got home, she wasn't surprised to find the ninth rose waiting for her. She picked it up carefully, her breath fogging in the cold air as she untied the note. The words met her with a tremor of warmth, a quiet echo of something she hadn't dared to believe.

"You are worthy."

Her chest tightened as she stared at the note, her fingers

trembling. Worthy. The word felt impossible, like it belonged to someone else entirely. She had spent so long convincing herself she wasn't—that her mistakes, her failures, her doubts had stripped her of any worth she might have had.

And yet, the words were here, written plainly, as if they were undeniable.

She brought the rose inside, adding it to the vase with the others. Nine now. Each one carrying a message that felt like a puzzle piece she couldn't quite put together.

The rest of the day passed in a haze. Anna cleaned the apartment, rearranging the same clutter she always ignored. She thought about the note, the word worthy repeating in her mind like the ticking of a clock. It didn't feel true, but it didn't feel entirely false either. It felt... possible.

She thought about the baby again. The life inside her didn't care about her doubts, her mistakes, her fears. It didn't measure her worth the way she did. It simply grew, steady and sure, a quiet reminder of something beyond herself.

Her phone buzzed with a text from her mother.

"Hi, sweetheart. Just wanted you to know I'm praying for you today. You're so loved. ❤"

Anna stared at the message, her throat tightening. Her mother's love had always been constant, unwavering, even when Anna felt like she didn't deserve it. Maybe that was what worthiness meant—not something you earned, but something you were given. Something you already had.

She typed a reply before she could overthink it.

"Thanks, Mom. I needed that today."

Catherine's reply came almost immediately.

"Always here for you, Anna. Always."

The words settled in her chest like a gentle warmth, pushing back the coldness that had lived there for so long.

That night, Anna sat at the table, the ninth rose cradled in her hands. She turned over the notes in her mind—the messages, the hope they had quietly awakened within her. She thought about her mother, about Beth, about the baby. And, hesitantly, about herself.

She spoke the words aloud, her voice unsteady but resolute.

"You are worthy."

They didn't feel entirely true—not yet. But they no longer felt out of reach, and for now, that was enough.

Chapter 10

December 21 | Forgiven

∞∞∞

T he apartment was still, the low hum of the heater the only sound as Anna sat on the edge of her bed, the morning light soft against the walls. Nine roses stood proud in the vase on the kitchen counter, their presence both comforting and unsettling. Each one seemed to carry a message she hadn't fully embraced but couldn't ignore.

She rested her hand on her womb, her thoughts drawn again to the baby. The reality of it pressed closer every day, insistent and unavoidable. It wasn't just the physical sensation—it was the haunting pull of the decision she still hadn't made. The truths from the roses lingered in her heart, quietly urging her forward, though the fear of her inadequacy felt louder.

When she opened the door, the cold air bit at her skin, sharp and relentless. She stepped onto the landing, her eyes immediately finding the tenth rose. Its crimson petals rested on the black mailbox, vivid against the frost. She reached for it, her fingers brushing the cool stem, its delicate weight grounding her in the stillness of the moment.

And then, before she unfolded the note, it was as though a small light pierced the shadowed corners of her soul, revealing both the depth of the darkness she had been living in and the existence of light she hadn't dared to hope for. It was like fumbling in a vast, uncharted cavern—hands brushing against cold stone, searching blindly for an exit—when the faintest glimmer broke through a hidden crack. Not blinding or overwhelming, but gentle and sure, it was enough to awaken her to the possibility of something beyond. Beyond the words. Beyond the roses. Beyond herself.

Words. It occurred to her that words like "love," "trust," and "forever" had unraveled her faith in their promise, fraying her at the seams until she felt hollow, broken. But these roses kept appearing, mysteriously, persistently, orchestrating a quiet symphony that softened her doubt. Much like a child's anticipation of presents on Christmas morning. Her heart was beginning to anticipate the words before she even opened the door. She was starting to yearn for them. And in that yearning, something deeper was awakening: a fragile, flickering belief.

She glanced at the rose in her hand and felt its solemn persistence mirroring something within her. Like the roses, these words were becoming real. Like the life within her. A tender gust of grace breaking through the darkness, drawing her toward something she couldn't yet name but felt she desperately needed.

She couldn't shake the feeling that someone understood what she needed before she did. That someone believed for her when she couldn't.

With eager anticipation she unraveled the familiar twine and unfolded the note. The words washed over her like a wave, both gentle and penetrating.

"You are forgiven."

For a long moment, she stood frozen, the note extending its solemn truth. *Forgiven*. The word was heavy and yet impossibly light, pressing against the rawest parts of her heart. It touched wounds she hadn't let herself acknowledge, places she thought had long since hardened. A whisper rose from the depths of her soul, fragile but insistent:

"Lord, help me to believe."

More than words, *meaning* lingered as she moved through the day, the note tucked carefully into her coat pocket. At work, the office buzzed with holiday chatter, but Anna barely registered it. Her mind was elsewhere, turning over the note's message like a stone in her hands.

She thought about her mistakes, the choices that had led her here. She thought about Tayler, his words of love that had turned hollow, the note he'd left behind. "I'm sorry." It hadn't felt like apology. It had felt like abandonment.

And then there was her family. Her mother's quiet, patient love, her father's distant but steady presence. Could they forgive her? Did they even think there was anything to forgive?

The question that scared her most was whether she could forgive herself.

When she got home, the roses greeted her like old friends. She ran her fingers over their petals, the messages lined up beside them on the counter. She took the newest note from her pocket, her eyes scanning the words again.

"You are forgiven."

The ache in her chest deepened. Forgiveness had always seemed like something out of reach, a concept reserved for people stronger, better, holier than her. But the note didn't ask for strength or holiness. It simply offered the words, unconditionally, as though they had always been hers to claim.

Her phone buzzed, breaking the silence. She picked it up and saw a text from Paul.

"Hey Anna, just thinking about you. I know we haven't talked much lately, but I hope you know how much I care about you. Let me know if you need anything, okay?"

Anna stared at the message, her heart tightening. Paul had always been the softer one, the brother who reached out when others pulled away. She thought about calling him, but the thought felt too overwhelming. Instead, she replied.

"Thanks, Paul. That means a lot."

His response came quickly. "Always here for you, sis. Seriously, anytime."

She set the phone down, her chest heavy with the ache of unspoken words. Paul's kindness felt like another note, a faint echo of something she wasn't ready to believe.

That evening, Anna sat at the table with the newest rose in her hands. She thought about the baby, the quiet life growing inside her. She thought about her mother's texts, her father's silence, her brothers' reserved but steadfast presence. She thought about Tayler, his absence a shadow that still lingered.

But most of all, she thought about herself. The part of her that had carried guilt and shame for so long it had become a second skin. The part of her that couldn't imagine a world where forgiveness was possible.

She gave voice to a longing buried deep within her—a key she had carried without knowing, its purpose just now beginning to surface. Her breath wavered as the words broke free.

"You are forgiven."

The words danced on the edge of belief, elusive and uncertain. But they didn't feel impossible anymore. A spark of something she hadn't felt in years stirred within her—a lightness, a breath, a tender touch of grace.

In the the night's warm embrace, Anna placed her hand on her womb and let the words linger in her mind. Forgiven. It wasn't an answer. It wasn't a solution. But it was a beginning.

And for now, that was enough.

Chapter 11

December 22 | Enough

∞∞∞

The morning was still, a fragile quiet pressing against Anna's chest as if the world itself was holding its breath. She had hardly slept, the words "You are forgiven" echoing through the night, breaking through the long-hardened walls of her heart. Forgiveness felt like a word too vast for her to hold. How could something so profound belong to her?

She lay back against the headboard, her hand moving instinctively to her womb—a movement she barely noticed anymore, as if she were tethering herself to the life within. It was small, unseen, yet undeniably present, pressing against her doubt with the quiet persistence of its being. That thought alone moved her deeply: something so real, so alive, and utterly indifferent to her fears.

The roses had taught her to look for meaning in the ordinary. The words she found each morning were no longer just words; they had begun to bloom into truths she couldn't ignore. *Forgiveness. Worth. Love.* They boldly spoke across the chasm of her disbelief, daring her to let them in. And yet, she knew the gap between hearing them and truly believing remained wide.

When she stepped onto the landing, the icy, crisp air stung her cheeks. Her sleepy eyes scanned the mailbox. The eleventh rose waited there, its rich petals like a hearth, seemingly radiating a warmth of their own, daring the frost. Her fingers brushed its sturdy stem as she lifted it, feeling its delicate weight in her hand.

Before she even unraveled the twine, she paused, aware of how she was being gently drawn in by its growing familiarity. So much more than a routine, it was becoming something like a relationship. The roses, the words—they felt like the language of someone who truly saw her, someone who believed in her when she couldn't. They had become more than gifts; they were murmurs of grace, softly stirring a meaning she thought had been lost.

Her heart pounding softly, she unfolded the note. Its message was simple, like all the others, yet it pierced her with quiet precision:

"You are enough."

The words moved across her heart like a soft gust of wind. *Enough.* The syllables felt foreign, like a language she had once known but long forgotten. Years of broken promises and unmet expectations had unraveled her belief in words like this, leaving them hollow. Yet here they were, glowing like faint embers in her soul, rekindling what she thought had faded—bringing life to what seemed dead, truth to what had been shrouded in lies.

She stared at the rose, its crimson petals vivid and unwavering, and thought of the life she carried. Like the rose, the baby didn't measure her worth. It simply grew, steady and sure, a quiet reminder of something beyond herself.

And ever lingering was the question of *belief*—not something easily or quickly won, not automatic, but something alive, like any relationship, requiring constant tending. She recalled sailing with Beth's family at their lake house. A sailboat could be masterfully crafted, but without raised sails, without wind, it would never move. She felt the same.

From the day before, the prayer had woven itself into the ritual, as natural as reaching for the roses each morning. It wasn't loud. It wasn't even fully formed. But it was real.

"Lord," she breathed, her voice tender yet resolute, "help me to believe."

As Anna held the rose close, she felt the faintest spark of hope: a quiet reminder that belief, like a rose, could bloom even in the frost—fanned by grace and the courage to lift her sails to the waiting wind.

At work, the note stayed in her coat pocket, its presence a quiet reassurance she couldn't ignore. The office was buzzing with pre-holiday energy, but Anna felt detached from it all. She sat at her desk, her mind elsewhere, the words from the note looping through her thoughts.

You are enough.

She wanted to believe it, but the doubts came just as quickly. If she were enough, why had Tayler left? If she were enough, why did she feel like a failure in every aspect of her life? The questions weighed on her, pulling her deeper into herself.

By lunchtime, her emerging belief and doubt were battling again. The strain was too much. She stepped outside, the cold air biting at her skin as she walked aimlessly through the city streets. The holiday decorations in shop windows felt like a cruel joke, their cheerfulness a stark contrast to the ache inside her.

Her phone buzzed in her pocket. She pulled it out and saw a text from her mother.

"Hi, sweetheart. I just wanted you to know how proud I am of you. You're stronger than you think, and I love you so much. ❤"

Anna stopped walking, her breath catching. The word hit her again. *Stronger.* Reverberating from her fifth rose from days ago. As if her mother's voice were echoing the same truths she couldn't yet believe. But desperately wanted to believe. And needed to keep hearing. Filled with a sense of wonder, she stared at the message for a long time before replying.

"Thanks, Mom. I love you too."

The response felt small, inadequate, but it was all she could manage. As she slipped her phone back into her pocket, she realized her hands were shaking.

That evening, Anna sat at the kitchen table, the eleventh rose in front of her. She stared at it for a long time, her thoughts churning. So much more than words, they were a challenge, a call to see herself differently. To believe. But she didn't know how.

Her hand moved to her womb again, resting there as she closed her eyes. She thought about the baby, the life she carried. She thought about the decision she hadn't made yet. You are enough. Could it be true for the child? Could it be true for her?

Tears welled up as the questions overwhelmed her. She felt the fractures in her armor widening, the walls she had built around herself crumbling. Her guilt, her fear, her shame—it all pressed down on her until she couldn't hold it anymore.

The sobs came suddenly, wracking her body as she buried her face in her hands. She cried for the choices she had made, for the love she had lost, for the life she didn't know how to protect. She cried for the girl she used to be and the woman she was now, broken and unsure.

When the tears finally subsided, Anna sat in the quiet of her apartment, the ache in her chest replaced by a strange stillness. She looked at the rose again, its beauty undiminished, and reached for the note. Her fingers brushed the words as she whispered them aloud.

"You are enough."

The words felt like a balm, but tentative and fragile, but real. She didn't believe them entirely, not yet. But she returned to the small opening within her, the tiny crack where the light persisted, soft and unyielding.

As the world outside settled into a peaceful hush, she turned inward, her hand resting gently on her womb, she spoke the words again, her voice steadier, the truth of them edging closer. And as sleep softly claimed her, they lingered like a tender promise, fragile yet growing, a hope she dared to believe might one day be hers.

Chapter 12

December 23 | Brave

∞∞∞

The day began like so many others, but something felt different. Anna couldn't place it at first. The apartment was as quiet as always, the snow outside blanketing the world in soft stillness. Yet there was a shift, subtle but unmistakable, as if the air carried something new—something alive.

She stood at the kitchen counter, her gaze resting on the roses. Eleven now, each one bearing a truth steadily wearing down the walls around her heart. *You are not alone. You are known. You are loved. You matter.* The words no longer hovered as distant questions; they lingered instead as gentle invitations, stirring a fragile sense of possibility.

When she opened the door, the twelfth rose was there, resting on the mailbox like the others. Its very presence had become something she now regarded as almost celestial, seeming to vanquish the gray of the morning. She stepped out into the cold, her heart stirring with a quiet anticipation of the warmth she knew was waiting.

By now, she had come to expect the roses, but her anticipation wasn't just about finding them—it was about being found. Each morning, as she reached for the next rose, it felt less like a ritual and more like a conversation. The roses and their words seemed to know her better than she knew herself, meeting her in places she hadn't yet dared to acknowledge.

As she untied the note, a tranquil stillness enveloped her, the cold biting at her skin. For a moment, she paused, her breath forming soft clouds in the air, before unfolding the message.

"You are brave."

The words resonated, not just as a statement but as a call—a reminder of something she hadn't thought possible for herself. *Brave.* It wasn't a word she would have used to describe herself. Most days, fear and uncertainty clung to her, their cruel, sharp barbs shouting down hope. Yet, as she read the note again, the word seemed to join all the others, reverberating in a quiet symphony, fragile but insistent.

The roses, the notes—they were a kind of solemn heartbeat, steady and sure, moments of quiet communion, pulling her closer to something she couldn't yet name but was beginning to trust. Like the life within her. She knew her inadequacy; she understood the sense in which she was "enough." She had the capacity to know she needed something more, to see the cracks of light breaking through her darkness.

Standing there in the cold, the twelfth rose in her hand, Anna raised her sail, lifting the prayer that had become part of her mornings. Her voice faltered slightly as she gazed at the snow-covered world, the words fragile but true.

"Lord, help me to believe."

The prayer wasn't about certainty but about surrender, a recognition that she couldn't bridge the gap alone. As the words left her lips, she felt the faintest stirring of that wind, carrying with it the promise of something greater.

Inside, she placed the twelfth rose gently in the vase with the others, each bloom a testament to the quiet persistence of love and grace. Twelve roses. Twelve heralds of truth, breaking through the fog of her fear.

"You are brave," she murmured to herself, testing the words. They didn't feel entirely true, but they didn't feel impossible either. And that was enough.

The day passed in a blur of tasks and half-hearted attempts at work. But the words on the note stayed with her, like a quiet drumbeat beneath her thoughts. *You are brave.*

What did it mean to be brave? She didn't feel brave. She felt afraid, beleagured, lost. But maybe bravery wasn't the absence of fear. Maybe it was the decision to move forward anyway, even when the path wasn't clear.

Her phone buzzed with a text from her mother.

"Hi sweetheart. I'd love to see you tomorrow. Let me know if you have time for coffee. 💜"

Anna stared at the message, her chest tightening. She thought about Catherine's unwavering presence, her quiet love that had never faltered. She thought about the baby, the secret she had carried alone for weeks. The idea of sharing it no longer felt impossible. It felt... necessary.

She typed a reply before she could talk herself out of it.

"Okay, Mom. Let's meet tomorrow morning."

Catherine's response came quickly. "Wonderful. I can't wait to see you. I love you so much."

Anna set the phone down, her heart pounding. She wasn't sure what she would say, but she knew it was time to say something. The words on the notes, the quiet pull of the roses—they had been leading her here, step by step, toward a moment she couldn't avoid any longer.

That evening, Anna sat at the kitchen table with the twelfth rose in her hands. She thought about the baby, the life she carried.

She thought about her mother, her brothers, Tayler. She thought about herself.

She gave voice to the words from the note, her tone steady but pining for their strength.

"You are brave."

They didn't feel entirely true, but they didn't feel impossible either. Something shifted within her—a quiet stirring, tentative yet resolute, a small but undeniable yes.

That night, as she lay in bed, her hand on her womb, Anna let the word brave linger in her mind. It no longer carried the weight of terror it once had; instead, it felt like the faint crack of light widening into an open door. What had been a distant glimmer in the suffocating dark now streamed through with radiant warmth, illuminating the hidden corners of her soul. The light carried not just clarity, but the quiet promise of something beautiful taking root within—a dignity she had long forgotten, a beauty she hadn't dared to claim, and a warmth that whispered of life not only growing beneath her hand but within her spirit.

And as she drifted off to sleep, she felt the hope that tomorrow would bring something new. Something real. Something she was ready to face.

Chapter 13

December 24 | Communion

∞∞∞

T he morning sunlight crept into her room slowly, brushing against the walls with a soft, golden glow. Anna sat on the edge of her bed, her hands resting lightly in her lap. Her heart fluttered with nervous anticipation. Today was the day she would meet her mother. She had agreed to coffee, and though the thought of revealing her secret terrified her, there was also a strange, serene sense of readiness.

Before leaving her room, she peeked out the front door. The mailbox stood empty, its black metal glistening under a light dusting of snow. For the first time in nearly two weeks, there was no rose waiting for her.

Anna stared at the mailbox, her breath misting in the cold air. The absence struck her like a sudden stillness after music fades— a pang of disappointment, sharp and undeniable. But as she stood there, the feeling shifted into something softer, almost reverent. Twelve roses. A dozen. It felt whole, as though the circle had closed.

Twelve months in a year. Twelve apostles. Twelve Days of Christmas. Twelve, a number of perfection and completion.

She smiled faintly, her fingers brushing the edge of the doorframe. The roses had been so much more than she'd ever expected. They were a grace she hadn't known how to ask for, a beacon that had carried her through the darkest days. Their absence now wasn't emptiness but a gentle invitation—a call to deeply know—even more, to *become*—the messages they had left behind.

You are loved. You are enough. You are brave.

The words, once distant and almost impossible to believe, had taken root. They were no longer just faint echoes written on scraps of paper. They were truths, stirring within her, asking to become her.

Anna closed the door softly, her thoughts circling around what she had learned. Belief wasn't static or passive—it was alive, asking her to move, to cooperate. The roses had been the wind, but now it was her turn to raise the sails.

She stood in the stillness of her apartment, her heart lifting with the prayer that had become her anchor. This time, it came not from desperation but from a yearning to step fully into the light that was breaking through her darkness.

"Lord," she whispered, her voice lifting with steady resolve, "help me to believe. Help me to carry these words within me."

As the morning stretched before her, Anna felt the faintest stirring of peace, a quiet certainty that the roses had been a gift to prepare her for this moment. They had brought her this far, but now, it was time to walk forward.

The world outside shimmered under the snow's gentle touch, and as she gathered her things to leave, Anna carried with her the silent reminder: the gift of belief wasn't given to be held—it was meant to be lived.

She arrived at the café a few minutes early, her eager hands curling around the coffee cup as if to steady the tremor within.. The place was warm and inviting, the smell of freshly brewed coffee and cinnamon mingling with the faint buzz of holiday chatter. She kept her gaze on the table, her thoughts racing.

When the door opened and Catherine walked in, Anna's heart pounded in her chest. Her mother's presence was as steady as it had always been, her movements calm and deliberate as she approached the table. Catherine's smile was warm but tinged with something deeper—something Anna hadn't seen before.

"Hi, sweetheart," Catherine said softly, sitting across from her. "I'm so glad you came."

Anna nodded, unable to speak at first. She stared at the cup in her hands, the words she had rehearsed crumbling beneath the loving depth of her mother's gaze.

Catherine reached across the table, her hand resting gently on Anna's. "Take your time," she said. "I'm here."

The kindness in her voice broke something open in Anna. Tears welled up, spilling over before she could stop them. "Mom, I —" Her voice cracked, and she shook her head, the words stuck in her throat.

Catherine's grip on her hand tightened, grounding her. "It's okay," she said, her own eyes glistening. "Whatever it is, it's okay."

Anna took a shaky breath, her free hand moving instinctively to her womb. The movement didn't go unnoticed, and Catherine's eyes softened, understanding glimmering across her face.

"Anna," she said gently, her voice unsteady. "Are you...?"

"I'm pregnant," Anna blurted, the words tumbling out before she could stop them. "I just found out a few weeks ago. Tayler—he —he's gone. I don't know what to do. I'm so scared, Mom."

The floodgates opened then, the words spilling out in a rush. She told Catherine everything—the roses, the notes, the guilt and shame she had carried, the decisions she had avoided. Her mother listened quietly, her expression a mixture of sadness and unyielding love.

When Anna finally stopped, her breath hitching, Catherine reached across the table and cupped her face in her hands. "Oh, my sweet girl," she said, her voice breaking. "I am so, so proud of you."

Anna's brow furrowed. "Proud? Of what? I've messed everything up."

"No," Catherine said firmly. "You haven't. You're here. You're trying. And you're carrying a life—a beautiful, precious life. That's something to be proud of, Anna. That's something sacred."

The words struck deep, breaking through the walls Anna had built around her heart. She let out a sob, leaning into her mother's touch. Catherine pulled her into a tight embrace, holding her as though she could shield her from the world.

When they returned to the family home later that day, Anna felt the familiar mix of comfort and apprehension. The house was warm, the faint smell of pine and baked goods filling the air. Her father, Michael, was in the living room, his usually stoic expression softening when he saw her.

"Anna," he said, standing as she entered. "It's good to see you."

The words were simple, but they carried a pull Anna hadn't expected. She hesitated, unsure of how to respond. Catherine placed a gentle hand on her back, encouraging her forward.

"Michael," Catherine said, her voice steady, though her eyes shimmered with unshed tears. "Anna has something she wants to share."

Anna swallowed hard, a faint tightness gripping her chest. Her gaze shifted to her father. Michael stood by the fireplace, his posture tall, his presence strong as ever, but his eyes softened as they met hers. She hesitated, the gravity of the moment holding her fast.

"Dad," she said, her voice barely above a whisper. "I'm... I'm pregnant."

The words hung in the air, heavy and fragile. For a moment, there was silence. Michael's face remained still, unreadable, as if he were turning the words over in his mind. Then, something in him broke. His eyes glistened, the stoic mask slipping away to reveal a tenderness Anna hadn't seen in years.

Michael stepped forward, his movements slow and deliberate, his eyes locked on hers. Anna felt her breath catch as she saw something in his face that she hadn't seen since she was a little girl—a raw vulnerability, a love so deep it almost broke her. When he knelt before her, taking her hands in his, she couldn't stop the tears that welled in her eyes.

"Anna," he said, his voice solemn, heavy with emotion, overcome with an inexpressable love. "You're carrying a life—a part of you, and a part of us. And you... you're a mother."

The words struck her like lightning, their power and truth wrapping around her. She stared at him, stunned by the honesty and pride in his voice. "You're a mother," he said again, this time with even more certainty, as though he were etching the words into her soul.

A sob broke from Anna's chest, and she covered her face with her hands, overcome. "Dad," she managed, her voice cracking, "I don't know if I can do this."

Michael reached up, gently pulling her hands away from her face so he could meet her eyes again. "You can," he said firmly, his voice steady despite the tears spilling down his cheeks. "Because you're not doing it alone. You have us—you have me."

Then, with a tenderness that shattered every wall she had built, Michael leaned forward and placed his hands gently over her womb. Bowing his head, his voice resonant and steady, he spoke to his unborn grandchild. "And I know you and I are going to be the very best of friends."

Anna's heart broke open. In that moment, the years of distance, silence, and unspoken words between them seemed to melt away. She reached down, covering his hands with hers, her tears falling freely as she whispered, "I think you will."

Michael looked up at her, his face streaked with tears, his eyes full of love and promise. Rising to his feet, he pulled her close, his embrace strong and steady, as if shielding her from every hurt she had ever known.

"You're moving back here," he said, his tone gentle but resolute. "This is your home. We'll take care of you and this baby together— no rent, no bills—just you, us, and this new life we've been given."

Anna hesitated, shaking her head. "Dad, I don't want to be a burden."

Michael pulled back just enough to look her in the eyes, his hands resting firmly on her shoulders. "You could never be a burden," he said, his voice low but full of conviction. "You've carried so much on your own already. It's time to let us carry some of it with you."

Catherine stepped beside them, placing a hand on Anna's back. "He's right, sweetheart," she said softly. "We want to do this. We need to do this."

Anna looked between her parents, her vision blurred with tears. Their love enveloped her, steady and unyielding, a shelter she hadn't realized she needed. She let herself lean into it, a quiet surrender. "Okay," she said softly, her voice veiling a jubilation she couldn't quite name. "Okay, I'll move back. Thank you. Thank you both."

Michael kissed the top of her head, his tears falling freely now. "No, Anna," he said, his voice breaking. "Thank you. Thank you for trusting us. For letting us be a part of this gift."

Anna's tears fell, unburdened by fear or sorrow. They carried hope, love, and the quiet stirrings of a healing she hadn't thought possible. She rested her head against her father's chest, his heartbeat strong and steady beneath her cheek, and she felt a safety she hadn't known in years.

That evening, as the family gathered around the Christmas tree, Anna felt something shift inside her. The weight of her guilt and fear hadn't disappeared, but it no longer felt insurmountable. Surrounded by her parents, the arms that gave her life, and nurtured her through life, she began to see herself through their eyes—not as a failure, but as someone loved and forgiven. Someone brave. Someone worthy.

As she glanced at the mantel, her eyes fell on the creche set. The empty manger stood at the center, waiting for the Christ child to arrive. Anna's gaze lingered on the figure of Mary, her serene face full of quiet strength.

Anna felt a connection she hadn't before—a shared understanding of fear, of uncertainty, of the courage it took to say yes to life.

Her hand moved to her womb, her heart full. She felt unseen streams of grace rising within, gently shaping themselves into a tender declaration.

"I'm ready."

Chapter 14

December 25 | Hallowed

∞∞∞

The house was quiet in the early morning, the hush of Christmas settling over everything. The snow outside lay pristine and untouched, the world still holding its breath before the day began. Anna woke early, the kind of waking where dreams linger, blending into the softness of reality. She stretched in her childhood bed, feeling the warmth of the quilt her mother had laid over her the night before.

When Anna came downstairs and stepped into the family room, a solemn quiet settled over the space, heavy with something unspoken. Paul, who had arrived earlier, stood with a grin that broke through the tension like sunlight dispersing lingering clouds. For a moment, she froze, struck by the sheer reality of him—no longer a voice over the phone or a fleeting text, but flesh and blood before her, bringing with him a sure connection to her roots, reaching deep into an unseen source of strength, something she hadn't realized she'd been missing. He crossed the room in a few strides and pulled her into an embrace that radiated warmth and undying affection, his presence dissolving shadows that had lingered far too long.

"There she is," he said, his voice low and rich with emotion. "Merry Christmas, Anna."

"Merry Christmas," she whispered, her arms wrapping tightly around him, returning the embrace as if it were something she'd been waiting for without knowing it. The strength of his presence —of being seen, held—was overwhelming, and for a moment, she marveled at how they'd grown so distant. How had something so vital, so human, been reduced to flickers of communication across a screen?

As they parted, her gaze swept the room, landing on her father's steady eyes, his quiet warmth anchoring her. Catherine was next, her smile glowing as she reached to pull Anna into a hug that held the tenderness of all the moments they had missed. In the power of their presence, Anna felt the lingering echoes of the roses—those messages of love, worth, and bravery now embodied in the people before her. The events of the day before had begun to thaw the cold cell of her isolation; in this moment, she was experiencing the stirring of wonder: here, in this home, was a family she hadn't realized she could still belong to.

"You look radiant," her mother whispered, brushing a strand of hair from Anna's face. "How did you sleep?"

"Well," Anna said honestly. "Better than I have in a long time."

They moved into the living room, where the fire crackled and the Christmas tree sparkled with twinkling lights. The creche set stood on the mantel, the manger now filled with the figure of the Christ Child. Anna's gaze lingered there, her heart catching as she thought about Mary again—the young mother who had faced her fears with quiet courage, choosing life in the midst of uncertainty.

After breakfast, as the family exchanged gifts, Michael placed a small box in Anna's lap. She looked up at him, surprised. "Dad, you didn't have to—"

"I wanted to," he said, his voice soft but firm. "Open it."

She carefully untied the ribbon and lifted the lid to reveal a delicate gold pendant hanging from a fine chain. It was a simple design: a single rose etched with intricate detail. Her fingers trembled as she held it up.

"It's beautiful," she whispered.

Michael's eyes glistened. "It reminded me of you. Strong, beautiful, and full of grace—even when you don't see it."

Tears welled up in Anna's eyes, but this time, they weren't from sorrow. They were from something new, something fragile but real growing in formidability—belonging. She slipped the pendant around her neck, the weight of it settling over her heart like a promise.

The morning continued to move with a sacred stillness, the kind that only Christmas morning could bring. The soft strains of carols played in the background, their melodies weaving gently with the flickering glow of candles set throughout the house. The scent of cinnamon and pine lingered in the air, mingling with the faint traces of freshly brewed coffee from breakfast. A hushed quiet settled over everything, as though the world itself had paused in reverence. After the warmth of gift-giving faded and the house grew still, Anna found herself drawn to the den.

The twelve roses waited there, their presence a silent sentinel. She paused in the doorway, her breath catching as her gaze fell upon them. The arrangement seemed to shimmer faintly in the morning light, their vivid petals daring the frost outside. Thoughts from the day before reverberated in her heart as if spoken by an unseen voice, filled with such tender love, beckoning her to make the connection. *Twelve months in a year. Twelve apostles. Twelve... enough.*

She traced the edge of a petal with her finger, the memories of the past weeks rising to the surface—the weight of her decisions, the whispers of the roses, the words that had begun to breathe life into her again.

You are loved. You are brave. You are enough.

Her fingers moved to the pendant resting on her chest, the one her father had given her, its petals so lifelike, it seemed to shimmer with a hidden light. He hadn't known about the other roses, hadn't known what they had meant to her. And yet, here it was—a gift that felt like it had come from the same mysterious place, the same unseen hand.

Anna smiled faintly, her fingers closing around the pendant. Her thoughts wandered, quiet and searching. She didn't know who had left the roses. She had wondered, of course. But now, she found she didn't need to know. Perhaps it wasn't meant to be known. The messages had arrived when she needed them most, and that was enough.

She drew one from the vase, holding it gently in her hand. The soft petals brushed against her fingers, but as she turned the stem, a thorn pricked her thumb. She winced, a small bead of blood welling on her skin. She didn't pull away, though. Instead, she stared at the thorn, at the contrast between its sharpness and the rose's beauty.

Just then, her father popped his head in the door, his eyes twinkling as he noticed her holding her blood-stained finger up with a rueful smile. "The price of beauty!" Anna said, the words escaping her with a new kind of vulnerability, as though speaking them aloud was an act of trust.

Michael stepped into the room, his footsteps soft on the hardwood floor. He moved toward her with quiet purpose and sat down beside her, resting his arm lightly across her shoulder. He spoke, his voice warm and familiar. "A rose wouldn't be a rose without its thorns."

She added words they had both discovered while reading about roses in her early childhood. "They protect it, keep it alive. There's something in that."

His grin broadened, delight and pride lighting his face. He squeezed her shoulder gently. "That's my wise one," he said, invoking the name he used to call her when she was little. The sound of it wrapped around her like a favorite blanket, warm and grounding.

Anna felt a lump rise in her throat but didn't speak. Instead, she leaned into his side, letting his embrace anchor her. She let herself drift back to the days when she was small, curled up with him on the couch as he read to her, calling her wise beyond her years whenever she asked a question that surprised him. The memory brushed against her heart like a familiar melody, both tender and bittersweet.

In that moment, words gave way to something greater, a solemn, grand silence settling between them—a communion of souls where neither needed to speak. It was the kind of intimacy that only grows when walls come down, when both are content simply to *be* in one another's presence. The weight of love, unspoken but deeply felt, passed between them like light through a windowpane, illuminating truths too vast and sacred for words. It wasn't merely comfort; it was connection—a meeting of hearts that recognized not just a shared history, but a shared home. In that quiet, they both understood: this wasn't just enough. This was everything.

Her thoughts turned inward, quiet and deep, flowing like a river below the surface. The roses had been all of it—beauty and hurt, joy and struggle,

She thought of the messages—the love, the courage, the quiet assurance they had given her. She thought of the pain she had carried, the doubts, the fears. And she thought of the life growing inside her, fragile and strong all at once. The roses had been all of it—the beauty, the hurt, the promise.

She thought of the figure of Mary in the creche, her serene face turned toward the tiny Child in the manger. Mary had known beauty, and she had known pain. She had carried life and carried sorrow, both held together in a way that felt achingly familiar.

That afternoon, as the family lingered in the living room, Catherine approached Anna with a quiet suggestion. "I called Father Moretti to ask if he'd be available to hear my confession after morning Mass, before the final Christmas Mass this evening," she said softly, settling beside her daughter. "He mentioned that other parishioners had asked as well, so he's set aside some time. Would you like to join me?"

Anna hesitated, her heart tightening at the thought. She hadn't been to confession in years—not since she had begun to feel so unworthy, so far from the grace she had once believed in. The idea of standing before a priest, laying bare all the choices she had made, felt terrifying. And yet, somewhere deep within, she remembered the relief she had felt in her younger years—the strange and powerful way confession had once lifted the weight from her soul.

"I don't know if I can," Anna said, her voice barely a whisper. "I don't even know where to start."

Catherine reached for her hand, her grip warm and steady. "You don't have to know," she said. "You just have to go. Let grace do the rest."

Anna looked at her mother, her throat tightening. Catherine's eyes held no judgment, only love—a love that mirrored the gentle awakening Anna had experienced through the roses. She nodded slowly, her voice soft with hesitant acceptance. "Okay. I'll go."

The church was solemn, the only sound the soft murmur of the Fr. Moretti's voice and the occasional shuffle of feet echoing through the sacred expanse. Anna sat in the pew, her hands clasped tightly together as she waited her turn. Her heart pounded, her mind racing with thoughts of what to say, how to explain the mess she had made of her life. But then, as the door to the confessional opened a strange calm came over her.

She stepped inside, the dim light casting gentle shadows across the small, quiet space. Kneeling, she made the sign of the cross, her trembling fingers brushing her forehead. Father greeted her with a warm, steady presence, inviting her to unburden her heart.

At first, her words came slowly, each admission heavy with hesitation. But as she continued, it was as though that single pinpoint of light had shattered the darkness entirely; a radiant, consuming light flooded her with a peace she had never experienced before—an inner calm and resolve that defied her understanding.

She spoke of her fears, her doubts, her mistakes. She laid bare the shame that had held her captive, the hollowness that had weighed her down for so long. And as the words poured forth, they felt less like wounds and more like offerings, lifted toward the light that now surrounded her.

And then, in the stillness of that sacred space, she heard Father Moretti's voice again—gentle, steady, imbued with the same grace she had once known but had long forgotten. He spoke of God's love, His boundless mercy, and the way He never ceased reaching for her, even in her darkest moments. When he pronounced the words of absolution, something deep within Anna shifted. The burden she had carried for so long was lifted, replaced by a lightness she had never thought possible—majestic and freeing, like the sail of a great ship unfurling its sail toward the heavens.

When she left the confessional, Catherine was waiting for her in the pew. Anna sat down beside her, her cheeks damp with tears, and whispered, "Thank you." Catherine simply smiled, taking her hand as they knelt together to pray.

That evening, the family attended Christmas Mass together. The church was aglow with candlelight, the air thick with the scent of evergreen and a hint of incense. The choir sang softly, their voices rising like a prayer. Anna knelt, her hands resting lightly on the pew. The words of the Gospel washed over her, the story of a child born into the world, fragile but carrying the enormity of eternity.

Beyond anything she had ever known, more than she could have ever expected, she felt a fullness in what she was hearing. It was real. All of it. The Word made flesh. The light in the darkness. The Savior who had come not for the perfect, but for the broken— for her.

As she glanced around the church, her gaze fell on the figure of the Christ Child in the creche. Her thoughts turned inward, quiet and deep. Like the manger, she had been empty, hollowed out by fear and shame. But now, she felt filled—by grace, by forgiveness, by love.

And she knew that this was the greatest gift of all.

A serene realization settled over her, like the gentle falling of snow. The roses had been from Him all along. Not directly, perhaps, but through the hands and hearts of others, through whisps of grace she hadn't seen until now. Every word, every message, every petal—each one had been His way of showing her what had always been true.

Back at home, the soft glow of Christmas light imbued the walls with a solemn radiance, wrapping the space in an unseen, tender embrace, their gentle patterns mirroring the quiet stillness that had settled over her heart. In her hand, she held the last rose, its thorn pressing lightly against her skin—a reminder of the strange and beautiful journey that had brought her here. She thought of the simple, powerful words that had accompanied each rose. They had pierced her doubts, lit her darkness, and become lanterns guiding her through the shadows.

It amazed her—the power of words. How they could wound or heal, empty or fill. These words—*Loved. Brave. Enough.*—had not just spoken to her but had reshaped her. They had softened the jagged edges of her pain and breathed life into the hollow spaces she had once thought beyond repair. They carried the promise of a love deeper and truer than she had ever dared to imagine.

And now, as she stood in the stillness of Christmas night, surrounded by light and grace, she saw the truth of it all—the beauty and the thorns, the wonder and the pain. The roses had been a gift, but they were only the beginning. Every word she had clung to, every truth she had struggled to believe, pointed her to the one Word—the Word made flesh. The Word who had stepped into her emptiness, not just to fill it but to transform it. The Word who had known her from the beginning, who had made her for Himself. He was the light that pierced the darkness, the life within her, and the love that had carried her through.

And then, no longer consumed by the hollow that had once haunted her—defined her, tormented her, and lied to her—a single word emerged, fresh and alive, evicting the pretender that had long ruled the throne of her heart. It came with a clarity, dignity, and unsurpassed grandeur, proclaiming the fullness, beauty, and truth she had now found—the truth of who she was, what she was, and, more profoundly, what she was becoming. Softly, yet with the weight of her journey, that word fell from her lips.

"Hallowed."

Questions for Consideration

Chapter 1: Alone

Theme: *You are not alone.*

Anna receives a note that reads, *"You are not alone,"* attached to a single rose. Struggling with deep loneliness after Tayler's departure, the message begins to stir a faint flicker of hope in her heart.

Scripture:

"I will never forsake you or abandon you." ~ Hebrews 13:5 (NABRE)

Questions:

1. How deeply do you believe that you are not alone, even in your most isolated moments?
2. What thoughts, experiences, or fears make it difficult for you to believe that you are not alone?
3. What steps can you take this week to more fully embrace the truth that you are not alone?
4. Who in your life might feel alone, and what will you do to remind them they are not alone?

Prayer:

Dear Lord, I renounce the lies that tell me I am truly alone. Break through my isolation and fill my heart with the truth of Your presence. Help me to be an instrument of Your love, reaching out to help someone truly know they are never alone. Amen.

Chapter 2: Known

Theme: *You are known.*

The second note reads, *"You are known,"* resonating deeply with Anna as she wrestles with feelings of being unseen and misunderstood. The words begin to challenge her feeling of invisibility.

Scripture:

"You have searched me, Lord, and you know me." ~ Psalm 139:1 (NABRE)

Questions:

1. How deeply do you believe that you are fully known and understood?
2. What fears, insecurities, or past experiences prevent you from believing you are truly known?
3. What steps can you take to trust that you are known by God and those who love you?
4. How can you show someone else in your life that they are seen and known?

Prayer:

Dear Lord, I renounce the fear and shame that make me hide who I truly am. Help me to rest in the truth that I am known completely and loved fully by You. Use me to affirm the value of another by seeing them as You do. Amen.

Chapter 5: Strength

Theme: *You are stronger than you think.*
The fifth note, *"You are stronger than you think,"* challenges Anna's perception of herself. It gently pushes her to consider the resilience she has shown, even in difficult times.

Scripture:
"I have the strength for everything through him who empowers me." ~ Philippians 4:13 (NABRE)

Questions:
1. How deeply do you believe that you are stronger than you think, even when facing difficulties?
2. What fears or false beliefs hold you back from recognizing your strength?
3. What is one way you can act with courage and strength in your current situation?
4. Who in your life needs encouragement to see their own strength, and how will you offer it?

Prayer:
Dear Lord, I renounce the lie that I am weak or incapable. Show me the strength You have placed within me and help me trust in Your power working through me. Empower me to encourage others to know and embrace their God-given strength. Amen.

Chapter 3: Loved

Theme: *You are loved.*

The third note, *"You are loved,"* touches Anna in a way that her aching heart desperately needs. She wrestles with doubts about her worthiness of love, but the message begins to plant seeds of reassurance.

Scripture:

"I have loved you with age-old love; therefore I have continued my faithfulness to you." ~ Jeremiah 31:3 (NABRE)

Questions:

1. How deeply do you believe that you are loved, regardless of your mistakes or weaknesses?
2. What lies, wounds, or barriers keep you from fully believing you are loved?
3. What practical steps can you take to open your heart to love this week?
4. How can you intentionally show someone else that they are deeply loved?

Prayer:

Dear Lord, I renounce the lie that I am unworthy of love. Help me to embrace the truth of Your unconditional love for me and let it overflow in how I love others. Make me a witness to Your love for those who are longing to feel and truly know it. Amen.

Chapter 4: Matter

Theme: *You matter.*

Anna receives the fourth note, *"You matter,"* a message that feels both foreign and desperately needed. As she begins to reflect on her own value, the words chip away at her self-doubt.

Scripture:

"For we are his handiwork, created in Christ Jesus for the good works that God has prepared in advance, that we should live in them." ~ Ephesians 2:10 (NABRE)

Questions:

1. How deeply do you believe that your life matters and that you have intrinsic value?
2. What doubts or external pressures make it hard for you to believe that you matter?
3. What actions can you take to remind yourself of your worth and purpose?
4. What will you do this week to affirm someone else's worth and value?

Prayer:

Dear Lord, I renounce the lie that I am insignificant. Help me to trust in the truth that my life matters deeply to You. Equip me to affirm the value and purpose of others around me. Amen.

Chapter 6: Meaning

Theme: *You mean something.*
The sixth note, *"You mean something,"* resonates with Anna as she contemplates the purpose and significance of her life. It moves her to question her doubts about her impact on the world.

Scripture:
"Before I formed you in the womb I knew you, before you were born I dedicated you, a prophet to the nations I appointed you." ~ Jeremiah 1:5 (NABRE)

Questions:
1. How deeply do you believe that your life has meaning and purpose?
2. What obstacles, such as past failures or self-doubt, make it hard to believe your life has meaning?
3. What steps will you take this week to live with greater purpose and meaning?
4. Who in your life needs reassurance that their life has meaning, and how will you offer it?

Prayer:
Dear Lord, I renounce the lie that my life is meaningless. Help me trust in the plans You have for me and live with intention. Use me to remind others of their unique purpose and value. Amen.

Chapter 7: Story

Theme: *Your story isn't over.*
Anna receives the seventh note, *"Your story isn't over,"* offering her a glimpse of hope. This message challenges her to believe in the possibility of redemption and new beginnings, even in the wake of past pain.

Scripture:
"The one who began a good work in you will continue to complete it until the day of Christ Jesus." ~ Philippians 1:6 (NABRE)

Questions:
1. How deeply do you believe that your story is not over and that new beginnings are possible?
2. What guilt, regret, or fear makes it hard to believe in new chapters for your life?
3. What step can you take this week to begin writing a new chapter in your story?
4. Who in your life needs to hear that their story is not over, and how will you encourage them?

Prayer:
Dear Lord, I renounce the lie that tells me my story is finished. Help me to trust in the new beginnings You offer and to embrace the hope of tomorrow. Use me to inspire hope in others who feel stuck in their story. Amen.

Chapter 8: Seen

Theme: *You are seen.*
The eighth note, *"You are seen,"* begins to heal Anna's feelings of invisibility. It reassures her that she is valued and noticed, even in her struggles.

Scripture:
"You are God who sees me." ~ Genesis 16:13 (NABRE)

Questions:
1. How deeply do you believe that you are seen and valued just as you are?
2. What experiences or lies make it hard to trust that you are truly seen?
3. What is one way you can act with confidence, knowing that you are seen and valued?
4. How will you let someone in your life know that they are seen and appreciated this week?

Prayer:
Dear Lord, I renounce the lie that I am invisible or overlooked. Help me to know that You see me fully and love me completely. Empower me to affirm the presence and value of others in my life. Amen.

Chapter 9: Worthy

Theme: *You are worthy.*

The ninth note, *"You are worthy,"* confronts Anna's deep-seated doubts about her value. It pushes her to consider that worthiness is not earned but bestowed by God's love.

Scripture:

"Because you are precious in my eyes and honored, and I love you."
~ Isaiah 43:4 (NABRE)

Questions:

1. How deeply do you believe that you are worthy of love and good things?
2. What shame, guilt, or wounds make it hard for you to feel worthy?
3. What is one step you will take this week to embrace your worthiness?
4. How will you affirm someone else's worthiness through your words or actions?

Prayer:

Dear Lord, I renounce the lie that I am unworthy of love and goodness. Help me to believe that I am worthy in Your eyes and to live from that truth. Make me a reflection of Your love, affirming the worth of others. Amen.

Chapter 10: Forgiven

Theme: *You are forgiven.*

The tenth note, *"You are forgiven,"* challenges Anna to let go of guilt and accept the freedom that comes from God's mercy. This truth begins to dismantle her feelings of condemnation.

Scripture:

"If we acknowledge our sins, he is faithful and just and will forgive our sins and cleanse us from every wrongdoing." ~ 1 John 1:9 (NABRE)

Questions:

1. How deeply do you believe that you are forgiven for your mistakes and failures?
2. What guilt, shame, or fear keeps you from accepting forgiveness?
3. What step will you take to embrace God's forgiveness in your life?
4. Who in your life needs your forgiveness, and how will you offer it?

Prayer:

Dear Lord, I renounce the lie that I am beyond forgiveness. Help me to receive the fullness of Your mercy and to walk in freedom. Teach me to extend the same forgiveness to others that You have shown me. Amen.

Chapter 11: Enough

Theme: *You are enough.*

The eleventh note, *"You are enough,"* speaks directly to Anna's insecurities. It encourages her to believe that her worth is not tied to her achievements or failures but rests in God's unchanging love.

Scripture:

"My grace is sufficient for you, for power is made perfect in weakness." ~ 2 Corinthians 12:9 (NABRE)

Questions:

1. How deeply do you believe that you are enough, just as you are, without having to prove yourself?
2. What insecurities or external pressures make you feel like you are not enough?
3. What can you do this week to rest in the truth that you are enough?
4. Who in your life needs to hear that they are enough, and how will you share this truth with them?

Prayer:

Dear Lord, I renounce the lie that I must earn my worth. Help me to know that I am enough because You have made me so. Use me to remind others of their inherent value and sufficiency in Your love. Amen.

Chapter 12: Brave

Theme: *You are brave.*
The twelfth note, *"You are brave,"* challenges Anna to see her courage not as the absence of fear but as her ability to move forward despite it.

Scripture:
"Be strong and steadfast! Do not fear nor be dismayed, for the Lord your God is with you wherever you go." ~ Joshua 1:9 (NABRE)

Questions:
1. How deeply do you believe that you are brave, even in the face of fear or uncertainty?
2. What fears or doubts make it hard for you to see yourself as brave?
3. What courageous step will you take this week to live out your bravery?
4. Who in your life needs encouragement to be brave, and how will you support them?

Prayer:
Dear Lord, I renounce the fear that grips me. Help me to live with courage and to trust in Your strength. Use me as Your instrument to inspire others to face their challenges bravely. Amen.

Chapter 13: Communion

Theme: *You belong.*

The thirteenth note, *"You belong,"* leads Anna to confront her feelings of disconnection and isolation. It reassures her of her place in the larger story of God's family and in the lives of those who love her.

Scripture:

"So then you are no longer strangers and sojourners, but you are fellow citizens with the holy ones and members of the household of God." ~ Ephesians 2:19 (NABRE)

Questions:

1. How deeply do you believe that you belong—to God, to others, to a community?
2. What feelings of rejection, isolation, or fear keep you from trusting that you belong?
3. What step can you take this week to strengthen your sense of belonging in your community or family?
4. Who in your life needs to know that they belong, and how will you help them feel welcomed and valued?

Prayer:

Dear Lord, I renounce the lies that tell me I am an outsider or unworthy of belonging. Help me to see the truth that I am a cherished part of Your family. Use me to foster belonging and connection in the lives of those around me. Amen.

Chapter 14: Hallowed

Theme: *You are sacred.*
The fourteenth note, *"You are sacred,"* reveals to Anna the truth of her inherent dignity and sanctity. It calls her to recognize her life as hallowed by God's presence and to see herself and others as reflections of His divine image.

Scripture:
"Do you not know that your body is a temple of the holy Spirit within you, whom you have from God, and that you are not your own?" ~ 1 Corinthians 6:19 (NABRE)

Questions:
1. How deeply do you believe that your life is sacred, created with divine purpose and dignity?
2. What doubts, struggles, or sins make it hard for you to see yourself as hallowed and set apart by God?
3. What is one way you will honor the sacredness of your life and body this week?
4. Who in your life needs to be reminded of their sacredness, and how will you affirm this truth to them?

Prayer:
Dear Lord, I renounce the lie that I am ordinary or unworthy of holiness. Help me to see my life as hallowed by Your presence, and to treat myself and others with reverence and love. Make me an instrument of Your grace, calling others to see their sacredness as Your beloved children. Amen.

Acknowledgements

There's a scene in *It's a Wonderful Life* that has always stayed with me, a moment that captures the profound truth at the heart of this book. George Bailey, played by Jimmy Stewart, stands at the brink of despair, convinced his life no longer matters. In his anguish, he is given an extraordinary gift: a vision of what the world would have been like had he never existed. Walking unseen through the town he's always known, George realizes the immeasurable impact of his life on others. What once seemed ordinary becomes extraordinary when seen through the lens of gratitude: for life, for relationships, and for the quiet, transformative difference we make simply by being present.

In that same spirit, I owe profound thanks to those who have shaped my life and this journey.

To my beloved parents, Bernie and Judy Schlueter: your love and attentive care have rippled through generations, from your children, to your more than fifty grandchildren, and into countless lives through the work we continue to create. Your steadfast faith and example of love have laid a foundation for a legacy that far surpasses anything we can measure.

To my beloved wife, soulmate, and best friend of nearly thirty years, Stephanie: more than my editor-extraordinaire, you are my anchor and my inspiration. Thank you for the exhilarating adventure of navigating our nature and mission in Christ through all of life's joys and challenges! You have been an effervescent embodiment of God's grace and love, our love overflowing into our seven uniquely gifted, wonderful, and virtue-refining children (one in heaven), their amazing spouses, and our growing legacy of grandchildren, a radiant testament to love and faith.

In this story, Anna experiences particularly transformative moments that have been attested to by countless souls throughout the ages, especially through the sacraments of Penance and the Eucharist. I wish to express my heartfelt gratitude for the extraordinary gift of priests, through whom God makes Himself present in the sacraments that bring eternal life. While priests are human, like all of us, their vocation carries a profound dignity that invites unique challenges and spiritual attacks beyond what we can fully comprehend. In my own life, I have been profoundly blessed to know countless priests whose unwavering devotion—heart, mind, body, and soul—reflects their deep love for God and His people.

The priest in this book is inspired by a beloved friend I have known since my early days discerning the priesthood while at Mount St. Mary's Seminary in Emmitsburg, Fr. Mark Moretti. He embodies the faithfulness and holiness I have witnessed in so many priests who continue to bless my life. As priests are essential to the healing and sanctification of souls, I invite you to join me in continually lifting them up in prayer and expressing gratitude for all who have touched your life.

To everyone who has been part of this journey, to the multitude who have inspired me and supported me, this book is a testament to your friendship and love, the beauty of relationship.

Above all, LORD GOD, I thank You, the source of all that is. You breathe purpose into our lives, sustain us through every trial, and call us to glorify You. In taking on flesh, You dignified our humanity, showing us that we are never closer to You than in our trials. Through every moment of discomfort and joy, You are weaving a story of purpose and fulfillment. Help us embrace our unsurpassed mission of making You, Who are Love, known.

About the Author

GREG SCHLUETER is a media producer, author, radio show host, and movement leader. Based upon his first book, "The Magnificent Piglets of Pigletsville," he's about fostering the convivial friendship of the Bourbies, passionate pursuit of the Scallywags, and the overall vibrant culture of Pigletsville. He lives in Holland, Ohio, with his wife, Stephanie, where they lead a movement committed to Someone leading us Somewhere guided by the Whisper of the Unseen. They are parents of seven with an ever-growing number of little Squigglesprouts. Enter the enchanting world of Squigglesprout.com.

Find out more about their movement: ILoveMyFamily.us. Listen to their weekly radio program and podcast: IGNITERadioLive.com. Follow Greg on Substack at GregorianRant.us.

PHOTO: Paul Lorei | Lorei Portraits

Publisher

Squigglesprout
BLOOMiNATION

SQUIGGLESPROUT is a media company founded in 2024. Our mission is to open souls to the horizon of the Good, Beautiful, True, and One through magnificent story telling. Find out more at Squigglesprout.com.

BLOOMiNATION. Bloom + Illumination + Nation.

"[A] word on Squigglesprout, the most enchanting floral wonder in all the world. In proportion to the sunlight bathing its delicate form, the mystical blue Squigglesprout hums a melodic tune which, amid its august company on a radiant summer day, becomes a chorus reverberating through the air. Each of its leaflets seems to sway in rhythm, adding a whimsical ballet to the garden's ensemble. Its sprightly nature draws others near, inviting them to partake in its infectious mirth."

   - The Magnificent Piglets of Pigletsville